D0167105

Chapter 1

It was Friday. School was over for the day.

And it was almost time for the big baseball game to start.

Carter High was going to play Maxwell High. The winner would go to the state finals.

Al played in right field. He could hardly wait for the game to start.

Al's real name was Alberto. But all of his friends called him Al.

Rey was his best friend. Rey played in center field.

Rey's real name was Reynardo. But all of his friends called him Rey.

Al said, "I still can not believe it. Win today. And we will go to the state finals."

"But first we must beat Maxwell," Rey said.

Al said, "I know, Rey. But we beat Maxwell twice. And by a lot of runs. Zack was the pitcher both times. And he will pitch today. So we should win."

Rey said, "Do not count on it, Al. We should win. But they could beat us. So we must keep our minds on this game. And not on the state finals."

It was time for the game to start. Carter High was the home team. So they went on the field first.

Al ran to right field. Rey ran to center field.

Troy ran with them. He played left field.

Maxwell didn't score in the first three innings. And Carter didn't score in the first two.

Zack led off the bottom of the third inning. He struck out. Zack was a good pitcher. But he was not a good hitter.

It was Al's turn to bat.

"Get a hit, Al," Rey yelled to him.

Al swung at the first two balls. And he missed. But then he got a hit to right field.

Troy was the next batter. Troy was a good hitter. But this time he struck out.

Rey was the next batter.

Al yelled to him. He said, "Hit a homerun, Rey. Hit a homerun."

Rey was a good hitter too. He had hit a homerun in all of the games.

Rey swung at the first ball and missed. He swung at the second ball and missed. But then he hit a homerun.

"Way to go, Rey," Al yelled to him.

All of the Carter guys yelled too.

The score was 2-0.

Carter scored three more runs in the fourth inning. But Maxwell scored four runs in the fifth inning.

It was the top of the last inning. Carter High was leading 5-4. As long as Maxwell didn't score one more run, Carter High would be in the state finals.

The first Maxwell player tried to bunt. But he got out.

"Out 1," the umpire said.

The next batter hit a grounder to third base. And he got out.

"Out 2," the umpire said.

Al was very excited. He said, "Just one more out, Rey. And we are on our way to the state finals."

The third batter hit a ball to right

field. Al did not get to the ball in time. But Al should have. He had been thinking about going to the finals. And not about the batter.

The ball hit a few feet in front of Al. Al got the ball. He quickly threw the ball to first base. But the batter got there before the ball did.

"I should have made that catch," Al said.

Rey said, "Don't worry about it, Al. Just think about the next batter."

The next batter walked. There were runners on first and second.

Al was glad there were two outs. But they should be out of the inning. And the game should be over.

The next batter hit the ball to right field. Al was back too far.

Could he get to the ball in time?

Rey yelled to Al. He said, "You can catch it, Al. Just keep your eyes on the ball."

Al ran as fast as he could. He got to the ball just before it hit the ground.

The game was over.

Carter High had won. The team was going to the state finals.

Chapter 2

The weekend went by slowly for Al. And so did the next week. All Al could think about was the state finals.

He could not keep his mind on his school work. So he was glad he didn't have to study for any tests.

Al was glad when Friday came. And school was over for the week.

He hurried to baseball practice. Rey was with him. It was the last practice before the state finals.

Al said, "I still cannot believe it. We are in the final four."

That was what Al had worked for

all season. And why he had practiced so hard.

All four teams were going to play the next day. Two in the morning. Two in the afternoon. Then the two winners would play to be the No. 1 team.

Al said, "Just think. This time next week we might be No. 1."

"We may be in the final four. But we still must win two games. We have to beat Hillman High in the first game. And they will not be easy to beat," Rey said.

They had played Hillman two times. And they had lost both games. Zack had been the pitcher.

Al said, "I know they beat us two times. And by a lot of runs. But Matt is going to pitch this time. So I think we can beat them."

Rey said, "I think we might too. Zack is a good pitcher. But I think Matt is better. I think he can beat Hillman."

Matt pitched OK at the start of the season. But he had gotten better. And now he pitched better than Zack.

Coach Karr blew his whistle. Then he said, "Team 1, you are the home team. Be ready to take the field in five minutes."

Al and Rey got their gloves. Then Al ran out to right field. Rey ran out to center field. And Troy ran out to left field.

The first batter for Team 2 struck out.

"Out 1," Coach Karr said.

The next batter hit a ball to the shortstop. He got out.

"Out 2," Coach Karr said.

Cruz was the third batter for Team 2. He was the back-up player for first base. He did not work hard at practice. So he was not on the first team. He didn't get to play much. But he did hit well when he played.

Rey called over to Al. He said, "You should back up some, Al. Cruz might hit a long one."

Al and Rey moved near the fence. So did Troy.

The first pitch to Cruz was a ball. The next two pitches were strikes. Cruz just looked at the two strikes. But then Cruz hit the next pitch to short right field.

Al had to run hard. But he got under the ball in time.

"Out 3," Coach Karr said.

Three boys up. Three boys down. Al hoped they had that good a start with Hillman.

Al and Rey started to run off the field. Troy did too.

"Way to go, Al," Troy said.

Rey said, "I am sorry I told you wrong, Al. I was sure Cruz would hit a long one."

Al had thought he would too.

"That is OK. I need to be ready for anything," Al said.

"We had better be tomorrow. That is for sure," Troy said.

Al said, "We will be. We are going to be No. 1 in the state."

"I don't know about that. We have to beat Hillman," Troy said.

"We can beat Hillman," Al said.

Al was sure they could.

Cruz heard the boys. He laughed. Then he said, "Sure we can. As long as they don't show up."

Al did not care what Cruz said. He was sure they could beat Hillman. But he was not sure they really would.

Chapter 3

Team 1 won the practice game 4-2. Then the boys practiced what they needed to work on. Some worked on how to hit. Some worked on how to catch and throw. And some worked on how to field the ball.

Coach Karr blew his whistle. Then he said, "Time to stop. All of you get over here."

The guys hurried to the coach.

Coach Karr said, "Be here by 7:15 tomorrow. We will leave at 7:30. Be on time. We won't wait for anyone."

"Not even for you, Coach?" Cruz asked.

Some guys laughed. But Al did not

think Cruz was funny.

Coach Karr looked at Cruz for a few minutes. Then he looked at all of the guys. He said, "We can't wait. We have to leave on time. We can't be late to the game. We would have to forfeit. And that is no way to lose a game. See you at 7:15."

The boys hurried into the gym. They quickly got ready to go home.

Al started walking out of the gym. Rey was with him.

Rey said, "Is Bel going to the state finals?"

Bel was Al's girlfriend. Her real name was Belinda. But all her friends called her Bel.

Al said, "I hope so. But she needs a ride. She thinks she can get one. I will call her when I get home. She should know then."

"I hope she can go. I know how much

you want her there," Rey said.

"That is for sure," Al said.

He always wanted Bel at the games to see him play.

Rey saw his ride.

Al said, "See you at 7:15, Rey. Don't be late. We know Coach Karr will leave anyone who is late."

Coach Karr had left a late player before.

Rey said, "I will be on time. And I will get a lot of rest."

"I will too," Al said.

But Al was not sure he would get a lot of rest. He was too excited about going to the state finals.

Al started to walk home. It wasn't long until he got to his house.

Al went in his house. It was time to eat. He wanted to call Bel right then. But he had to eat.

Al ate quickly. But he still could not call Bel.

First he had to talk to his mom and dad. They wanted to talk to him about the state finals. They wanted to go and see him play. But they had to work.

The three talked for a while. Then Al called Bel.

Bel answered the phone.

"Did you get a ride?" he asked.

Bel said, "Yes. Sue said she will take Paz and me."

Sue was Matt's girlfriend. And Paz was Bel's best friend.

Paz liked Cruz. But she and Cruz did not date.

Bel said, "I am so excited. I can hardly wait to get there. And for the first game to start. Sue thinks we will beat Hillman. All because Matt will pitch. But I think we will win because of you."

That made Al feel very good.

Al and Bel talked for a while longer.

Then his mom came in the room. She said, "You must not stay on the phone so long, Alberto. You must rest for the games."

Al wanted to keep talking to Bel. But he knew he should get off the phone. He still had some things to do before he went to bed.

"I must go, Bel. I will see you at the game," Al said.

Al did what he had to do. And then he went to bed.

He could hardly wait for the next morning to come.

Chapter 4

Al got up at 6:00. He ate quickly. Then he hurried to the school. He got there about 7:00. Rey got there at the same time. Al was glad to see Rey was early too.

Most of the players were there. Al saw Troy and Zack. And he saw Matt. But he did not see Cruz.

Al was glad Matt was there. He had been sure Matt would be on time.

Al said, "I still cannot believe it. We are going to the state finals."

"I can hardly believe it too," Rey said.

Al went over to Coach Karr. Rey went

over to the coach with him.

"You can check me off, Coach Karr," Al said.

Coach Karr had a list of the team. He put a check by each player when the player got there.

"You can check me off too," Rey said.

Cruz came up behind them. He said, "And me too, Coach."

By 7:15 all of the boys were there.

Soon they would be on their way to the game.

Al could hardly wait to get on the bus. He was ready to get there and start to play.

Coach Karr blew his whistle. All the boys quit talking. They walked over to Coach Karr.

Coach Karr said, "Think about what I have told you. About how to hit and throw. And how to catch and field.

Keep your mind on the game. You can win. But you have to play hard."

Al could hardly wait for the Hillman game to start. He was glad the game was in the morning. And not in the afternoon.

Coach Karr said, "And don't forget this. Make me proud. Try your best to win. But play fair. Only a fair win is a good win."

It was time to go. The boys got on the bus. Al and Rey sat together. Troy and Cruz sat behind them.

Matt and Zack sat with Coach Karr. He wanted them to sit with him. So they could talk about the hitters on the other three teams.

The bus started to go. The team was on its way to the state finals.

Al said, "All the hard work this year was worth it."

"It sure was," Troy said.

"Yes. It was," Rey said.

"I am not so sure it was," Cruz said.

Al was not surprised Cruz said that. He knew Cruz didn't like to work hard. That was why Cruz was not on the first team.

Al said, "Maybe it was not for you. But it sure was for me. And I can hardly wait for the first game to start."

"Do not get your hopes up too high, Al. We might lose," Rey said.

"I know. But I think we can win," Al said.

"I think we might too. But I am not as sure as you are," Rey said.

Cruz said, "I don't think we will win. They have beat us two times."

"But Matt will pitch this time. So it will not be the same," Troy said.

Troy was Matt's best friend.

Cruz said, "Maybe not. And maybe

Hillman will not show up. Then we can win by a forfeit."

Cruz laughed.

Cruz thought that was funny. But Al did not think it was.

The boys rode for a while and did not talk.

Then Cruz said, "I know one thing for sure."

"What?" Al asked.

"Coach Karr was wrong," Cruz said.

"About what?" the other three boys asked at the same time.

"About only a fair win is a good win. Any win is a good win. A win is still a win. Fair or not," Cruz said.

Al did not think Cruz was right.

Al wanted to win. But he wanted it to be a fair win.

It would not be a real win unless it was a fair win.

Chapter 5

The bus trip took two hours. There was some road work. And the bus had to stop a lot and wait.

Al was glad they left early.

It was a long bus ride. And Al was glad to get off the bus.

"I thought we would never get here," Rey said.

Al felt the same way.

Some fans from Carter High were there. They had on the school colors. Some fans from Hillman were there too. And they had on their school colors.

But the Hillman team was not there.

Al had thought the team would be.

Al said, "Hillman is not here. I am glad we got here first."

Carter would have more time to get ready for the game. And they would have all the field for a while.

Al looked for Bel. But he did not see her.

Coach Karr said, "Warm up. But not too much. You don't want to get tired before the game starts."

Al and Rey ran out on the field.

Rey said, "Who do you think will pitch? Do you think it will be the kid who beat us two times?"

"Yes," Al said.

Rey said, "He is their best pitcher. You don't think their coach will save him for the second game?"

Al said, "No. Hillman has to win the first game. Or they will not be in a second game. The two teams this afternoon are good. But we will be harder to beat than them."

Rey said, "I think you are right about that. The two teams are good. But not as good as Carter High."

Some balls were hit to Al and Rey. They threw them back to the infield.

Then Al and Rey hit some balls.

More fans came. But Hillman still did not come.

And Al still did not see Bel. She should have been there by then. But he was not worried. He was sure Bel was late because of the road work. He hoped Bel would come before the game started.

Coach Karr blew his whistle. He said, "Time to stop."

Al and Rey started off the field.

Rey said, "Where is Hillman? They should be here by now."

"They should have been here when we got here," Al said.

Troy and Cruz came up to them.

Al said, "Hillman must get here soon. Or they will not have time to warm up. It is not long until time for the game to start."

Cruz laughed. Then he said, "Maybe they will not be here on time. And we can win by a forfeit. Then we might be No. 1. I think we can beat the other two teams."

Al said, "Who would want to win by a forfeit? I sure would not want to."

"And I would not want to," Rey said.

"And I wouldn't want to," Troy said.

"I would," Cruz said.

Al knew Cruz really would want to win that way. He was glad Rey and Troy were not like Cruz.

Chapter 6

It was almost time for the game to start. But Hillman was still not there.

Al saw a lot of people with Carter High colors on. There were not many with Hillman colors on.

Troy said, "A lot of people are here. I didn't think that many from Carter would come."

Al said, "I did. It is not every year the team plays to be No. 1."

The last time had been six years ago.

Al looked for Bel. But he did not see her. He was starting to worry about her.

Troy said, "Are you looking for Bel?"

Al said, "Yes. She said she would come to the game. But I do not see her. And I am starting to worry about her."

Troy said, "Sue is coming. And I don't see her. I hope she gets here before the game starts. Or Matt will worry about her. And not keep his mind on the game."

It would be the same with Al. He would worry about Bel. And not keep his mind on the game.

Some more fans came.

Cruz said, "I see a lot of girls. And most of them are here to see me play."

Then Cruz laughed.

Al thought Cruz just wanted the girls to see him on the team. And Al didn't think Cruz cared about playing in the games.

Troy said, "Oh, good. I see Sue. Now Matt will think only about the game. And not about Sue."

"Where is she?" Al asked. Al knew Bel would be with Sue.

Troy told him.

Al saw Bel. He waved at her. And she waved at him.

Now Al was ready for the game to start.

Some more fans came. But Hillman still did not come.

"Why do you think Hillman is not here?" Rey asked.

Al said, "I do not know. But there must be road work. And they had to stop for a while."

"They don't come the same way we do," Troy said.

Al said, "I know. But there may be work on their road too."

Cruz said, "They should have left early. Coach Karr made us leave early. So their coach should have made them leave early too."

For once Al thought Cruz was right.

Al looked over at the umpires. They were all standing near first base. They were talking. And they were looking at their watches.

The head umpire walked over to Coach Karr.

The boys quit talking. So they could hear what the umpire said.

The umpire said, "The Hillman coach just called. They had to stop because of road work. But they should be here any time now."

Al was right. That was why Hillman was late.

Coach Karr called all the players over. He said, "Hillman should be here soon. Are you all ready to play?"

"Yes," they all yelled at the same time.

Coach Karr said, "Keep your mind on this game. You can beat Hillman. Don't think about the second game. We have to win this one first."

Al could hardly wait for the game to start.

Al looked at the road. But he did not see the Hillman bus.

Some more people came. Some were Carter High fans. And some were Hillman High fans.

Rey looked at his watch.

Then Rey said, "It is time for the game to start."

And Hillman was still not there.

Cruz said, "Hillman is not here. So that means we will win by a forfeit."

Al was tired of Cruz saying that. So he said, "Be quiet, Cruz."

Al did not want to win by a forfeit. That would not be the right kind of win.

Cruz looked surprised.

Al looked at the umpires. They were

all standing near home plate. They were all talking to each other. They looked at their watches. They talked some more.

Then the head umpire walked over to Coach Karr. He said, "I thought Hillman would be here by now. They have 15 minutes. They must be here by then. Or you will win by a forfeit."

Coach Karr said, "I'm sure they will be here by then."

Al was sure they would be too.

Chapter 7

Some more Carter High fans came. And some more Hillman fans came. But the Hillman team did not come.

"They had better hurry. Or we will win by a forfeit," Troy said.

Cruz smiled. But he did not say anything.

Al kept looking at the road. But he did not see the Hillman bus.

Rey said, "It will not be long now."

The boys tried to talk about something else. But all they could think about was the game.

Rey looked at his watch. Then he said, "It has been 15 minutes."

Al looked at the umpires. They were all looking at their watches. Then they had a long talk with each other.

Cruz said, "Why are they talking so long? It has been 15 minutes. It is time they said Hillman has to forfeit."

Al said, "Do not be in such a hurry, Cruz. You are the only one who wants to win by a forfeit."

But Al was not sure Cruz was the only one.

Troy said, "I came to play. And I know Matt wants to pitch. Because he wants a chance to beat Hillman. But the umpires can't make us wait all day."

"They sure are trying to make us do that," Cruz said.

"No. They are not," Al said.

Al did not want to win by a forfeit. And he wished Cruz would stop talking about it.

The four umpires looked at their watches. They talked some more.

Then the head umpire went over to Coach Karr.

The Carter boys quit talking. So they could hear what he said to the coach.

The umpire said, "Hillman is not here. And the 15 minutes are up."

"Now it has been 25 minutes," Cruz said.

But only Al and Rey and Troy could hear him.

The umpire said, "This is a big game. We don't want to give a forfeit."

And Al didn't want them to. But he knew they would have to do it.

The umpire said, "But Hillman is very

late. So you have a forfeit, Coach Karr. I will tell the fans."

Cruz and some of the Carter boys yelled. But Al and Rey and Troy did not. And Matt and Zack did not.

The umpire went to tell the fans. But the Hillman fans started to yell before he could.

Al looked to see why they were yelling.

The Hillman bus was coming up the road.

Chapter 8

The Hillman coach quickly got off the bus. Then the team got off. Al could tell the boys were very excited. Just like he was.

The head umpire walked over to the Hillman coach. Al wished he could hear what they were saying.

"Do we still get our forfeit?" Cruz asked.

Rey said, "Yes. The umpire has already given it to us. He cannot take it back."

"Are you sure?" Cruz asked.

Rey did not answer.

The Hillman coach looked at Coach Karr. Then he and the umpire started to walk over to Coach Karr. Coach Karr went to meet them.

"What do you think they are saying?" Rey asked Al.

"I wish I knew," Al said.

The three men talked for a few minutes. Then Coach Karr walked back to the team.

He said, "Guys, I need to talk to you."

"Did the umpire take away our forfeit?" Cruz asked.

Coach Karr said, "No. But we need to talk about it."

"Why? What is there to talk about?" Cruz asked.

"The Hillman coach wants us to play them. And not take the forfeit. I told him it was up to you," Coach Karr said.

"What do you want us to do?" Al asked.

"What you think is right," Coach Karr said.

"We take the forfeit," Cruz said.

"Yeah," some guys said.

Al said, "But think about the Hillman players. Think about how they will feel."

"They wouldn't give up a forfeit to play us," Cruz said.

Al said, "Maybe not. But we do not know that for sure."

Coach Karr said, "It is up to you, guys. What do you want to do? Do you want to win like this?"

"Yes," Cruz said.

"A forfeit is not a real win," Al said.

Cruz said, "Sure it is. A win is a win. And a forfeit is a win."

"But it is not the right kind of win," Al said.

"All wins are the right kind of win," Cruz said.

"It is not fair to the Hillman players," Al said.

"And it wasn't fair for us to have to wait on them. We got here on time," Cruz said.

"Think about what other teams will say about us," Al said.

"What?" Cruz asked.

"That Hillman beat us two times this year. And that they would have beat us today," Al said.

"So? Who cares what they might say?" Cruz said.

Al said, "I do. And I rode for two hours on a bus. I did not ride that long to stand around all morning. I came to play."

"I'm with you. Let's vote," Troy said.

Coach Karr said, "Are you all ready to vote?"

"Yes," most of the team said.

"Do you want to play? Put your hand up for a yes," Coach Karr said.

Al and Rey and Troy quickly put up their hands. And so did Matt and Zack.

Most of the boys voted to play. But not all of them.

At first Cruz did not put his hand up. But then he said, "OK. I vote to play."

Cruz put his hand up. Then the other boys put their hands up. So then all of the boys had voted to play.

Coach Karr said, "Boys, I am proud of you. I knew you would not let me down. I knew you would do what was right. Now show those boys how to win. The right way."

Could they beat Hillman? Al thought they could. But he was not sure they would. But it was better to lose than to win by a forfeit.